This book belongs to

....

Peppa Pig™

LADYBIRD BOOKS

UK | USA | Canada | Ireland | Australia | India | New Zealand | South Africa

Ladybird Books is part of the Penguin Random House group of companies
whose addresses can be found at global.penguinrandomhouse.com.

www.penguin.co.uk   www.puffin.co.uk   www.ladybird.co.uk

Penguin
Random House
UK

First published 2019
001

Printed in China

A CIP catalogue record for this book is available from the British Library

ISBN: 978-0-241-39247-8

All correspondence to:
Ladybird Books
Penguin Random House Children's
80 Strand, London WC2R 0RL

George
and the
Dinosaur

"Dine-saw, ROARRRR!" shouted George.
George and his friends Richard Rabbit and Edmond Elephant
loved dinosaurs. Wherever they went, they were always
searching for fossils, stones and bones.

In the sandpit . . .

at the playground . . .

and even in
Grandpa Pig's garden!

One day, when Richard and Edmond came to play, Mummy Pig had a special surprise.

"We're going on a fossil-hunting adventure at the beach," she said, "with Miss Rabbit the Fossil Hunter!"

"Are fossils always dinosaurs, Mummy?" asked Peppa.
"They can also be the remains of plants or animals from a long, long
time ago," explained Mummy Pig.

The children put on their fossil-hunting clothes and packed their bags with their special tools and fact books.

"Ready to go exploring?" Mummy Pig asked.

"YEESSS!" cheered Peppa, George and George's friends, jumping up and down.

The brave explorers set off to meet Miss Rabbit at the beach.

"The tide was high last night," said Miss Rabbit when they arrived. "Hopefully there'll be lots of wonderful things whipped up by the waves for us to discover."

"Yippee!"
cheered the children.

"But, if not, you can always buy fossils from my shop at the end," Miss Rabbit continued. "There's an offer on today . . . two for the price of one!"

Miss Rabbit took out her fossil collection to show the children.
"This swirly rock is an ammonite," she said. "And these shiny rocks
are called fool's gold." Miss Rabbit held up some little rocks with
gold bits in them.

"Oooh! Gold!" gasped Peppa. "I love hunting for treasure!"

"Unfortunately it's not real gold, Peppa," explained Miss Rabbit. "But it's lovely and shiny!"

"This one is a belemnite," said Edmond, looking at Miss Rabbit's fossils.
"It's an extinct mollusc. And I believe that one is fossilized poo."
"Eugh! Poo!" snorted the other children. "Hee! Hee! Hee!"

"Don't worry," said Edmond. "The poo is millions of years old!"
Edmond Elephant was very clever.
"Wow," said Miss Rabbit. "You really know your stuff, Edmond."

George pulled out a dinosaur book from his bag.
"Dine-saw, ROARRR?" he asked, showing
Miss Rabbit a picture of a dinosaur.

"No one has **ever** found a complete dinosaur skeleton
on this beach, I'm afraid, George," said Miss Rabbit. "But you
might find some little fossils like the ones in my collection."

Then Miss Rabbit turned to
them all and said, "Now . . .
shall we get started?"

Peppa walked along the beach looking at the ground, but she soon gave up. "I can't see **anything**, Mummy," she said. "Just lots and lots of sand and stones! I'm going to build a sandcastle instead."

Meanwhile, George, Edmond and Richard explored the beach together. They took their fossil-hunting mission **very** seriously.

After Peppa had finished her sandcastle, she peered over at George.
"Look, Mummy!" she called. "George has found something!"

Mummy Pig and Miss Rabbit looked over at George.
Their mouths dropped open.
The explorers were pointing to a HUGE
rock further down the beach!

"Oh dear, Mummy Pig," sighed Miss Rabbit. "It looks like you're bringing the whole beach home with you!"

"Hello, George," said Mummy Pig. "What do we have here, then?"
"Dine-saw," said George, holding his arms out as wide as they could go. "BIG dine-saw!"

"We believe this rock contains the complete skeleton of a dinosaur," explained Edmond. "George found footprints in the rocks near it, which are a clear sign. Can you help us crack it open, please?"
"Are you sure it's not just a big rock?" Mummy Pig asked.

But then Miss Rabbit took a
closer look at it and pulled out
her phone.
"Yes, that's right. Very big,"
she said into her phone.
"Please come immediately."

Soon after, Mr Rabbit arrived in a big truck with a team of helpers.
Very carefully, they lifted the rock on to the truck.
"We'll meet you at the museum," Mr Rabbit called out as they drove off.

At the museum, everyone watched excitedly as
Mr Rabbit and his team cracked open the rock.

Everyone gasped!
Mr Rabbit was the first to speak. "What we
have here is a COMPLETE skeleton of a . . ."

"Dine-saw?" interrupted George.
"That's correct, it is a dinosaur. In fact,
it's a triceratops," confirmed Mr Rabbit.
"George, you are an expert fossil
hunter, aren't you? This is an amazing
dinosaur discovery!"

"WOW!" everyone cried, looking at the skeleton. Even Peppa was impressed.

"Now," said Mr Rabbit, "what shall we call this incredible dinosaur?"
"George-saw-us the first!" cried Peppa. "Because George saw the dinosaur first!"

"*ROAR!*" cheered George.
Everyone laughed. "Hee! Hee! Hee!"

"In that case, I officially name this dinosaur the George-o-saurus-ceratops-ROAR," announced Mr Rabbit. "A big dinosaur like this needs a big name like that!"

Everyone **loves** fossil hunting and dinosaurs!

Especially George the dinosaur expert!